First American edition

Text and illustrations copyright © Phillida Gili 1983
Idea conceived by Bettina Tayleur Ltd.

Published in 1984 by The Viking Press
40 West 23rd Street, New York, N.Y. 10010

Produced by Bettina Tayleur Ltd.
1 Newburgh Street, London W1V 1LH

Printed and bound in Italy by Sagdos S.p.A., Milan
for Imago Publishing Ltd.

Published simultaneously in Canada by
Penguin Books Canada Ltd.

1 2 3 4 5 88 87 86 85 84

Library of Congress Cataloging in Publication Data

Gili, Phillida.
 Fanny and Charles: a regency escapade or, the trick
that went wrong.

 Summary: In early nineteenth-century England,
Charles's prank with a mouse backfires during his family's
vacation in Bath.
 [1. Mice—Fiction. 2. Brothers and sisters—Fiction.
3. England—Fiction] I. Title.
PZ7.G397Fan 1984 [Fic]   83–5850
ISBN 0–670–30697–5

FANNY & CHARLES

A REGENCY ESCAPADE

OR

The Trick That Went Wrong

PHILLIDA GILI

THE VIKING PRESS · NEW YORK

It was well past Fanny's bed-time and the hall candles had been lit. The flames flickered each time the front door opened and Fanny shivered as she peered through the banisters at the guests arriving. If only Charles hadn't told her so many ghost stories! She thought she could hear rustlings in the darkness behind her.

Just then the drawing room door opened with a burst of talking and laughter. This was the moment Fanny had been waiting for; she watched, fascinated, as her parents and their friends walked through to the dining room, their jewels sparkling in the candlelight. To her they were princes and princesses on their way to a ball.

FANNY

CHARLES

EDDIE

Once the door had shut, Fanny took a deep breath and raced for the safety of her bed.

The sight of her trunk in the moonlight filled her with excitement – in two days' time she would be in Bath!

'I wonder if you'll like living in a town?' she said to her dolls Lizzie and Jane, tucked up beside her. Before they could answer, a loud scuffling noise made her blood run cold. She dived under the bedclothes and lay rigid, listening intently.

Mice? Rats? . . . Ghosts?

Silence.

She peeped out from her bedclothes. Something white was drifting towards her and she watched, spellbound, to see if it would pass right through her trunk . . . . It didn't.

With a shriek of agony the apparition crashed headlong on to the floor. There was a brief moment of silence, then Fanny began to giggle helplessly, and once she started she couldn't stop.

'Fanny! Help me, quick!' said a muffled voice.

'Oh, do be quiet! You'll wake Eddie.' Too late. A thin wail was swiftly followed by heavy footsteps getting closer, and there stood their nurse in the doorway, candle in hand. Mrs Cork was not amused by what she found. In no time, Charles was back in his own bed, and peace was restored.

Next morning, Fanny's mother sent for her. She went with a heavy heart.

'Fanny, I am surprised at you,' said her mother. 'What were you and Charles thinking of?' Fanny bit her lip. 'I don't want any excuses. Instead of going out this morning, you can make yourself useful here.'

'Start by passing me that jewel box.

Then hand me those hats.'

Fanny sighed. 'It's not fair,' she thought bitterly.
'It's Lizzie and Jane's last chance to play
with the stable kittens before we go to Bath.'

Fanny thought her mother's packing would never end. The moment she was dismissed she ran to the stables. It was the last straw to find Charles there with one of the kittens on his lap.

'You've been here all the time, you lucky thing, while I've had to — '

'Lucky! *You* didn't have to see Father. Besides, I'm not allowed any lunch and I'm starving.'

'It serves you — ' But just then the bell rang for lunch and off she ran.

The sight of the gardener delivering vegetables
to the back door made Charles
feel even hungrier.
He actually found himself
longing for a raw carrot,
or even a lettuce leaf.
Suddenly he saw something
fall out of the basket.
The stable cat saw it too,
and pounced.
Charles forgot his troubles as
he snatched a tiny field-mouse
from the cat's paws.
While he looked at it trembling
in his hands, he was struck by a bright idea.
Why not hide it in Fanny's trunk? What a joke that would be!

Early next morning the family gathered in the hall. Charles hopped up and down with glee when he saw the footmen carrying Fanny's trunk out to the carriage.

'Fanny dear,' said her mother, 'Nurse is very busy, so please will you look after Eddie. He's going to trip someone up with his horse.'

'We don't want broken bones now, do we?' added Mrs Cork.

Fanny did her best, but Eddie wasn't as easy to manage as Lizzie and Jane. It was a relief when at last they were all seated in the carriage.

With a crack of the whip they were away. Eddie, lulled by the jolting of the carriage, soon fell asleep. He missed all the sights of the journey and only woke when they got stuck in the mud and everyone had to get out.

A pedlar approached them, followed by a crowd of children. She had a basket of ribbons and a hundred pretty things which Fanny longed for. As she reached for the penny in her string purse, she caught sight of a thin child hanging behind the others. Her face looked pinched and cold. Fanny bought a shiny red ribbon, gave it quickly to the little girl and ran back to the carriage.

Charles's day was made by the sight of a platoon of soldiers with swords dangling at their sides. They were exactly like his tin ones, except that none of them was broken!

Outside the town a phaeton overtook them. 'I hope we'll have one of those when we're in Bath,' said Charles, 'because I want to drive one.' 'Hmm,' said his father. 'Ghosts aren't supposed to be very good at that sort of thing.' Charles became unusually quiet – but not for long.

As they rattled through the crowded streets of Bath, Charles was on tenterhooks —
soon Fanny would be opening her trunk! They stopped at a tall, narrow house.
Fanny and Charles followed her trunk up and up, nearly to the top.

Fanny's shriek could be heard all over the house. She'd seen, quite clearly, a tiny mouse crouching between Lizzie and Jane.

'Don't be a baby,' said Charles, grinning. 'It's only a sweet little mouse.'

The mouse leapt out of the trunk and Fanny leapt on to a chair. She glared at her brother. 'You think you're clever to scare me, don't you? But what about the mouse? It might have suffocated!' 'What rot – ' Charles began. Then he stopped. He hadn't thought of that. The door was flung open and Mrs Cork strode into the room. 'There was a mouse in my trunk!' said Fanny. Mrs Cork turned pale. 'Oh dear, I'd better, er . . . go and get some help then,' she said, backing towards the door.

At last the plump figure of Mr Fish the butler surfaced, rather out of breath.

'Right-o, Miss Frances, where is 'e?'

'Under my chair. *Please* take him away!' begged Fanny.

But no mouse was to be found, and after a careful search Mr Fish went downstairs, defeated.

'You can stay on that chair all night if you like,' said Charles, 'I'm going to have my supper.'

Fanny was so angry that she chased him all the way downstairs. Neither of them had noticed a flash of brown race across the bare floorboards to her bed.

Fanny's first night in Bath was a restless one. It had begun to rain, which always made her gloomy. The endless grinding of carriage wheels kept her awake and made home feel very far away.

It was quite different in the morning. Fanny opened her shutters and sunlight flooded the room. She cheered up at once and reached for her clothes.

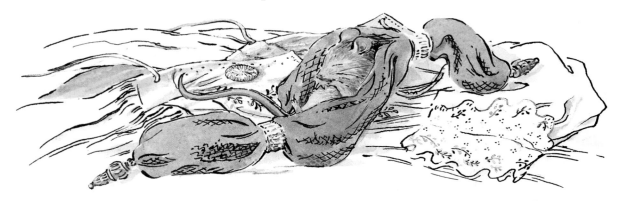

Her hand froze in mid-air. There, lying curled in her purse, was the mouse, asleep. Fanny had never seen anything so sweet.

'How on earth could I have been scared of you?' she wondered.

'You'll need something to eat when you wake up,' she whispered. She found the kitchen at the very bottom of the house. In a dark corner sat a large and malignant cat, which looked at Fanny with half-shut eyes. A kind scullery-maid gave her some bread and she raced back upstairs. Too late!

The mouse had disappeared again. Desolate, she ran to find Charles, who was astonished at her change of heart. They decided they must find him and make him their pet, to take the place of the kittens they'd left behind.

With Eddie trailing behind them they started their search in the attic and worked their way down the house. They peered under beds and in Mr Fish's boots. They looked in their mother's bonnets and even opened her best parasol. They examined their father's top hats and investigated his great-coat pockets. No luck. The cook's cat passed them on the staircase, looking dreadfully smug. 'What worries me,' said Charles, 'is that he's a field-mouse. He won't know how to look after himself in a town.'

It was bed-time when they heard
their mother's cry of alarm.

'Children! You'll never guess —
a little mouse just jumped
out of my jewel box!'

'Don't you worry, ma'am,'
said her maid, 'Cook's cat
William is an excellent mouser.
He'll soon polish him off.'
Fanny and Charles
looked at each other miserably.

The second day in Bath dawned as fine as the first, and Mrs Cork took the children to the park with their battledores and shuttlecocks. Fanny and Charles began to argue almost at once: 'It's my turn to begin.'

'No it's not, it's mine!'

Charles tried to snatch the basket from Fanny, but it fell to the ground and out rolled the shuttlecocks. Fanny stamped her foot. 'Why do you *always* –'
She broke off with a gasp. There, blinking in the sunlight, was the little mouse!

'Quick!' said Charles. 'Grab him before he escapes! Put him in your bonnet.'
But the mouse didn't wait to hear what treat was in store for him. Instead
he bolted into the bushes.

'Oh *no*!' said Charles. 'This time we've really lost him.'

'Perhaps he'll be happier here,' said Fanny. 'Don't forget he's a field-mouse.
He's used to out-door life.'

'But I did so want him to be my pet,' said Charles.

Back in the house, Fanny and Charles were greeted by William, purring in the hall. It was strange, but somehow he looked different, not malignant at all. He seemed quite friendly, really. Fanny paused to stroke his back as she went upstairs.